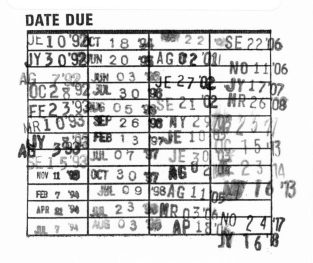

BLUE BUG VISITS MEXICO

by Virginia Poulet

Illustrated by Peggy Perry Anderson

CHILDRENS PRESS®
CHICAGO

Photographs on pages 18 and 19:

1. Some Mexican women wear a long shawl called a "rebozo."
2. Young boy plays his guitar for his friends.
3. Small shop in downtown Mexico City
4. Close-up of the carvings on the pyramid of Quetzalcoatl, an Aztec god
5. Fruits and vegetables are sold in open-air markets throughout Mexico.
6. Indian women from the state of Oaxaca weave cloth in a village square.
7. The National Cathedral in Mexico City.

Photographs on pages 22 and 23:

1. The church at Taxco was built more than 450 years ago.
2. Mariachi band plays in the floating gardens at Xochimilco in Mexico City.
3. Pyramid of the moon was built by the Maya Indians.
4. Two volcanoes stand outside of Mexico City.
5. Acapulco is a popular resort on the Pacific Ocean.

PHOTO CREDITS

© Eugenia Fawcett—23 (top)

Hillstrom Stock Photo—© D.J. VARIAKOJIS, 19 (top);
© RAYMOND F. HILLSTROM, 22 (top right)

© Alex Kerstitch—22 (left)

Root Resources—© BYRON CRADER, 19 (bottom center)

© Chandler Forman—18 (right)

SuperStock International, Inc.—18 (center and left),
19 (center left and center right), 22 (bottom right), 23 (bottom)

Library of Congress Cataloging-in-Publication Data

Poulet, Virginia.
　　Blue Bug visits Mexico / by Virginia Poulet;
illustrated by Peggy Perry Anderson.
　　　　p.　　cm. — (Blue Bug books)
　　Summary: In Mexico, Blue Bug enjoys looking at
the toys and crafts, watching people before the
fiesta, and dancing.
　　ISBN 0-516-03429-4
　　[1.　Mexico—Fiction.　2.　Insects—Fiction.]
I.　Anderson, Peggy Perry, ill.　II.　Title.
III.　Series: Poulet, Virginia. Blue Bug books.
PZ7.P86Bj　1990
[E]—dc20　　　　　　　　　　　89-25420
　　　　　　　　　　　　　　　　　CIP
　　　　　　　　　　　　　　　　　AC

In Mexico, Blue Bug

saw toys and crafts,

4

SILBATO

pottery, and

glass.

After lunch, Blue Bug

13

put his money into

his new piggy bank.

He took snapshots

and put stamps

on pretty postcards.

① ② ③

FRUTA

Cacahuates

He had a snack and

bumped into a cactus!

At the fiesta,

Blue Bug loved

learning

a new dance.